For Jan

M v H

First published in the United States and Canada in 2015 by Lemniscaat USA LLC · New York
Distributed in the United States by Lemniscaat USA LLC · New York

Cataloging-in-publication data is available.

ISBN 978-1-935954-39-2 (Hardcover)
Printed in the United States by Worzalla, Stevens Point, Wisconsin

www.lemniscaatusa.com

Uh-Oh Octopus!

Elle van Lieshout & Erik van Os

Mies van Hout

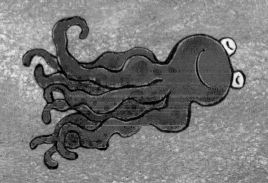

Lemniscaat

Octopus lived in a cozy home under the sea.

He had nothing to complain about.

He could make himself a decent meal.

He had a wonderful view.

But one morning,
when returning from his daily swim,
Octopus found a big tail blocking the entrance to his home.
"Oh no!" he exclaimed. "Look at that tail!"
The tail scared him. He swam away.

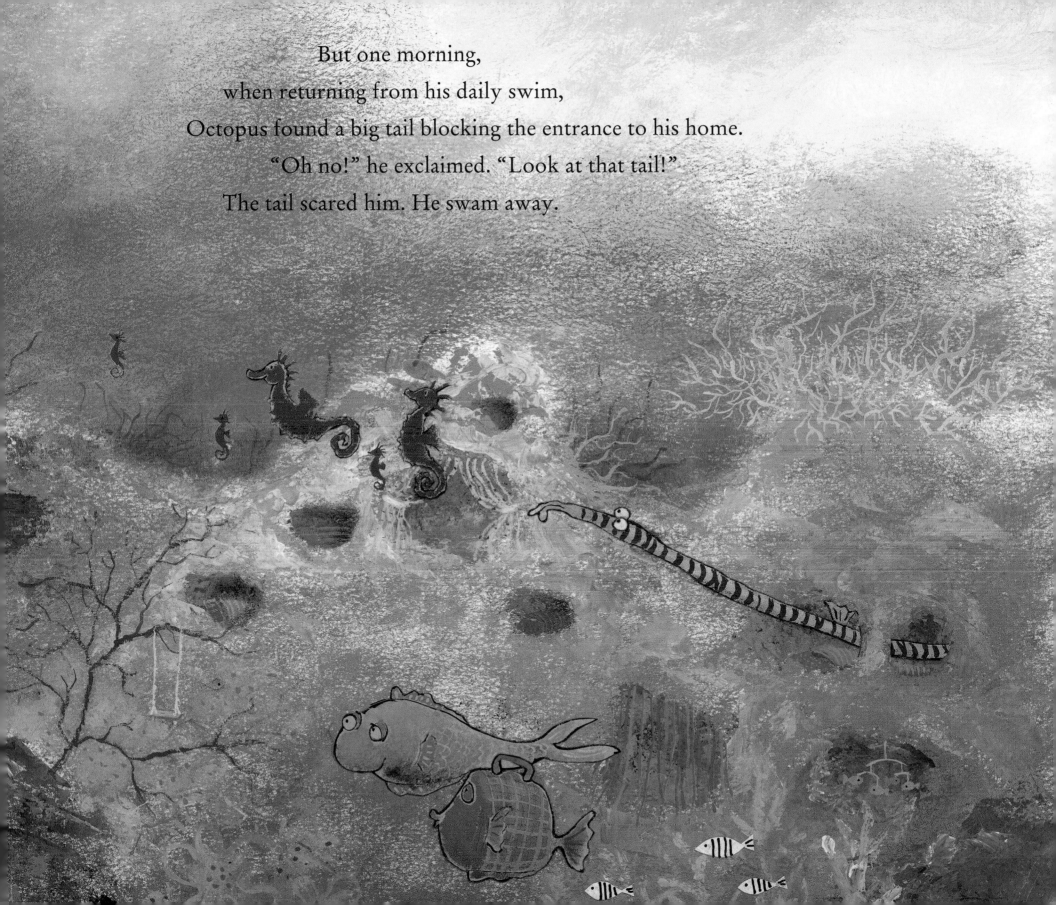

This had to be discussed with his friends.

Hermit Crab listened and sighed, "Well, well, an intruder.

Who cares? Just move to another place.

The sea is filled with opportunities."

Octopus shook his head. This didn't help at all.

The Jellyfish family—who had heard it all—suggested,
"There's only one thing that you can do!
Get rid of the stranger. Chase him away!"
Octopus thought about the large tail.
No, that was not a very good idea.

He swam off to ask Whale for advice.
Whale would probably have a huge idea.
Whale had no suggestions.
He didn't have a house, and, besides, he didn't need one.
He lived where he swam and never bothered
to make a home in one place.

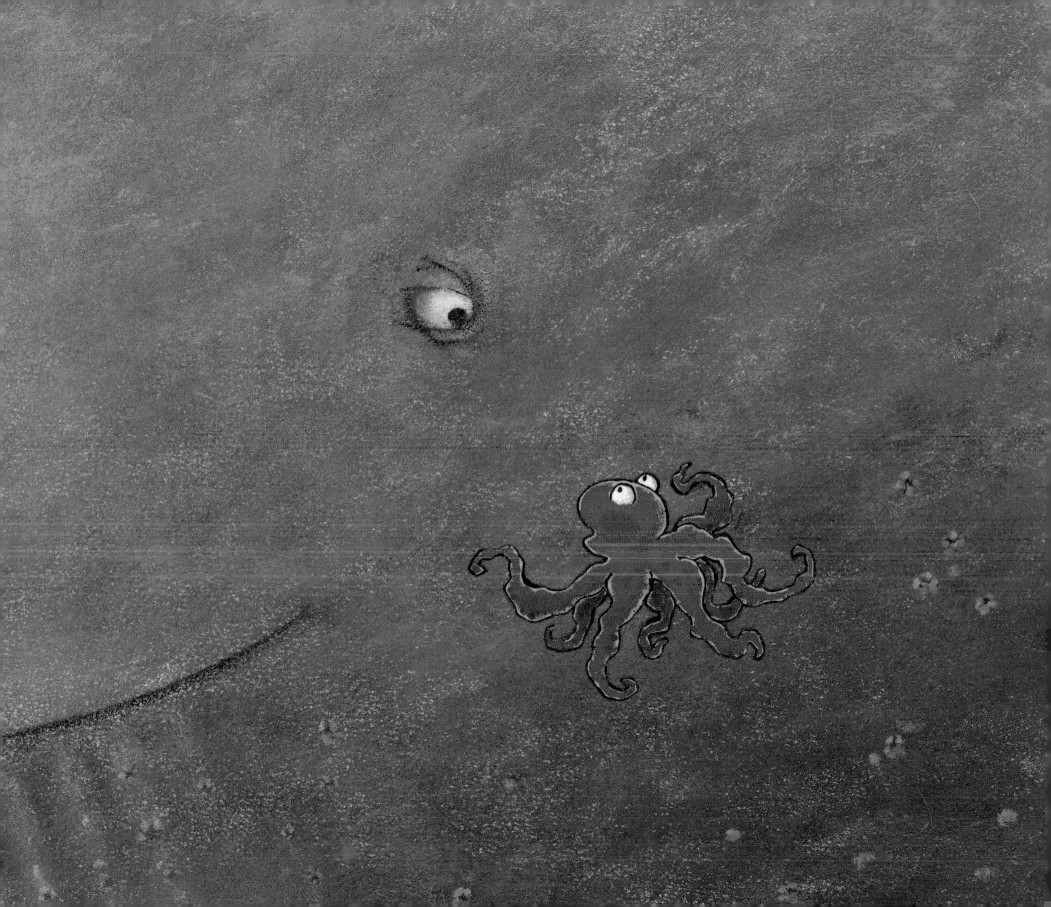

Octopus sank to the bottom of the sea where Reef Perch lived.

"Tell me," urged Reef Perch.

So Octopus told him about how he had discovered the intruder.

And that it was his house and

he had lived there for so many years.

How dared this stupid stranger take over the apartment

without even asking? If he wouldn't leave immediately

Octopus would—he would—

"Calm down," said his friend.

'Calm down?" exclaimed Octopus.

"As if that will help," he muttered.

And off he went.

He bumped into Lionfish, who snarled "What do you want?"
Lionfish showed his stings to impress Octopus.
"N-n-nothing sir," Octopus stammered.
"But there's a stranger in my home and I just don't know—"
"Get rid of him!" Lionfish snapped while keeping an eye
on Octopus. "Eat him! Swallow him!"
Octopus gulped, nodded, and swam away as fast as he could.

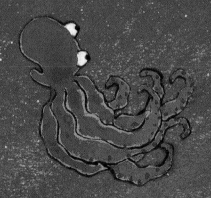

Now, all the sea animals knew about the tail.
Everybody suggested a different solution.

"Spit fire!" said Fire Fish.
"Sting him!" said Needle Fish.
"Sting him again!" said Sea Urchin.

"Cover him with slime," said Sea Snail.
"Pick up your stuff and move," said Trunk Fish.
"Declare war on him," ordered Soldier Fish.
Lantern Fish shone its light. Pajama *fish* yawned.

"Oh, no," Octopus moaned.
He started to feel nauseous.
So many fish with so many solutions.

He was seasick.

Everybody was saying
something else.
"But what do you want?"
Did he hear the sea
whisper?
"How about you?
What would you do?"

Me?, " asked Octopus. "Oh."
"Yes, what would I do?"

"I could go to the tail and ask him
politely to leave."

So he did. Octopus swam back
to his home.

Very cautiously, he knocked on the stranger's tail.
"My dearest sir," he asked gently,
"would you perhaps be so kind as to—"
"Help!" a tiny voice sobbed. "Please! Could someone
pull me out? I've been stuck for such a long time."
Such a huge tail and such a small voice!
With all eight arms, Octopus grabbed the tail and
pulled and pulled.
"HELP!" he shouted. "Will somebody please help?"

Everybody came to help him pull.

"Oh," Octopus blushed. "If I'd only known you were a lady! That's different!"

Was it the sea that had whispered to him?

Or his heart?